Let's Play Tag!

📖 Read the Page

▶ Read the Story

★ Game

★ Level 1   ★★ Level 2

☺ Yes   ☹ No

🔁 Repeat

⬛ Stop

💻

TinkerBell

Tinker Bell's True Talent

A new fairy had arrived in Pixie Hollow, and it was time for this little fairy to find her talent.

"How will I know what my talent is?" the fairy wondered.

But soon she knew. When the little fairy held the hammer, it began to glow. She was a tinker fairy now, called Tinker Bell!

Bobble and Clank explained that tinker fairies help all the other fairies prepare for spring. Tinker Bell was excited. She looked forward to visiting the mainland to help with spring's arrival.

But then she discovered that tinker fairies don't go to the mainland. Only the nature fairies do.

"There's got to be more to my life than just pots and kettles!" said Tink.

"Wait...if I can learn a nature talent, then I can go to the mainland for spring too!"

 So, Tinker Bell tried to be a water fairy.

"Let's put dewdrops on spider webs!" said her friend Silvermist, a very talented water fairy.

"You just cup your hands, reach into the water, and take a drop!"

Then, Silvermist delicately placed the water onto the web.

Tinker Bell carefully scooped up some water, but the drops kept bursting in her hands.

Tink clearly did
not have the talent
to be a water fairy.

Next, Tinker Bell tried to
be a light fairy. She had seen
Iridessa grab sunlight and toss
it at fireflies to make them glow.

But when Tink tried to toss
the light, it wouldn't fly
from her hand.

"This is impossible!" Tink
shouted, throwing the cone
of light to the ground.

The light bounced
around the field ...

...and landed on Tinker Bell!
The fireflies chased her into
the night.

Tinker Bell remembered seeing Fawn, an animal fairy, teaching baby birds how to fly. That couldn't be too hard, right?

"Smile and establish trust," she said nervously to herself.

"Hey!" shouted Tinker Bell. "You want to do some flap-flap today?"

The scared little bird shook his head.

"Just flap your wings," said Tink.

"Come on!" she shouted, but the
little bird struggled to get away.
It was too afraid to fly.

Tinker Bell sighed.
"This is not working."

Tinker Bell had not succeeded at any
of the nature fairy talents.

"I'll never get to the mainland!" said a
frustrated Tink.

Then she saw something shiny hidden in the leaves.

It was a box! But some of
the pieces that were supposed
to be inside the box were missing.

Tinker Bell found the lost pieces
and put the box together again.

 Tinker Bell needed one last piece. She found a lovely ballerina figurine that fit perfectly onto the box.

She turned the ballerina. It worked! She had repaired a music box!

Tink was overjoyed. She was doing what she loved. Tinkering really was her true talent!

When it was time for the nature fairies to go to the mainland for spring, Tinker Bell was given a wonderful surprise. She was to fly to the mainland too! Her task was to return the music box to the little girl who lost it.

Tinker Bell's dream came true as she flew off
to the mainland!

She had used her talent to fix the music box and
was able to return the lost treasure to a little girl.

Tinker Bell learned an important lesson:

*Always be true
to yourself.*

spring

both

winter

safety pin

hammer

beads

bell

coin

screw

spring

diamond